FIRE!

David Orme

Evans

Published by Evans Brothers Limited
2A Portman Mansions
Chiltern St
London W1U 6NR

© Evans Brothers Limited 2005

First published in 2005

British Library Cataloguing in Publication Data
Orme, David
Fire. - (Shades)
1.Great Fire, London, England, 1666 - Fiction
2.London (England) - History - 17th century - Fiction
3.Historical fiction
4.Young adult fiction
I.Title
823.9'14[J]

ISBN-10 : 023752922X

13-digit ISBN (from January 2007) 978 0 237 52922 2

Visit www.fireinteractive.co.uk to find out more about
the Fire of London
Evans Publishing Group are not responsible for the
content of external websites

Series Editor: David Orme
Editor: Julia Moffatt
Designer: Rob Walster

Cannon Street, London
Sunday 2nd September 1666
3 a.m.

I don't know what it was that woke me. It may have been the sound of shouting in the streets. I didn't usually wake up in the night. My master, John Brown, made sure that he got all the work out of me that he could so I didn't get a lot of sleep.

I lay there and listened. There was another sound as well as the shouting; drums were beating, far away in the night. I thought maybe the Dutch had arrived at last. There had been rumours of invasion for days. Maybe there would be fighting in the streets.

I slipped out of bed and opened the tiny

attic window. Straight away I knew what was happening. There was a stiff breeze from the east, and I could smell smoke. A fire. That was all. There was a fire somewhere or other most weeks.

I went back to bed, but it was hard to sleep. The drumming and shouting carried on. I began to smell smoke, even with the window shut fast. I got up and looked out of the window once more. This time, I could see a red glow in the sky. It was on the other side of the City, though. A long way off.

Then a great surge of flame swelled up. I found out later that flames had reached a warehouse full of barrels of pitch. It hadn't rained for days, and the whole City was tinder dry.

As I looked to the east, I thought about my twin sister. We were foundlings. Our mother had left us at the door of the church of St Martin Outwich. The parish looked after us and named us Martin and Martha Outwich, after the church. When we were old enough, I was apprenticed to Mr Brown, and Martha became a lady's maid. She looked after an old lady called Mrs Shaw in Seething Lane, near the Tower. I hadn't seen her for a month. My master rarely let me out of the house these days. He'd changed since last year's plague. His son, William had died, and now it seemed that he wanted me to suffer for it – because I was alive and William wasn't.

He had always been a hard master, but now it was much worse. Often these days the only supper I got was a blow to the head.

Once again I lay down, but it was a long time before I finally managed to sleep.

Seething Lane, London
2nd September 1666
4 a.m.

Mrs Shaw never left her bedroom. She had arthritis in her legs and so she could barely walk; she had become very fat in recent years and could no longer manage the narrow twisting stairs down to the ground floor. I slept in a little room nearby; I slept lightly, for the old lady could call at any time to be helped out of bed, perhaps to use the chamber pot, or just to be walked around the room for a little while to ease the cramps in her legs.

My room faced east, away from the City, so I knew nothing of the fire before she called me.

'Martha, come here!'

I wrapped my shawl around my shoulders and went in to Mrs Shaw's room. The old lady was sitting up in bed.

'Look out, girl. Tell me what's ado!'

I opened the window and looked out. I could hear drums and shouting, though faintly; the wind was blowing the sound to the west.

'There's a fire, Ma'am. I can see the flames of it.'

'Where?'

'Somewhere in the City. By the river, I think. It is a long way off.'

Somewhere in the City. That's where my brother Martin lived and worked. I hadn't seen him for over four weeks now. His master was a shoemaker, and trade had been poor since the plague. Martin never said so, but I was certain that he was being treated cruelly.

'Are you sure child? That it is a long way off?'

Mrs Shaw dreaded fire. She knew that if her house caught alight, there was little she could do to escape.

'A long way off, Mistress.'

She was wide awake now.

'Read to me, Martha.'

I was still sleepy, and longed for another hour in bed, but I had to do what Mrs Shaw asked. I took down the heavy Bible from the shelf and began to read aloud.

Cannon Street
2nd September 1666
6 a.m.

Bang!

'Get up, you idle wretch!'

Bang! Another blow across my head. I had overslept. Usually I made sure I was up well before my master.

I jumped out of bed. The shoemaker had opened the attic window and was looking out. The smell of smoke was very strong now. I could hear a new sound; the wild clashing of church bells.

I dressed quickly and rushed downstairs, hoping to get out of my master's way. The shoemaker's wife was already up and dressed. She was flapping about in her

11

usual hopeless way. Sometimes she was kind to me – but only when she thought her husband wouldn't notice.

Mr Brown came downstairs, ignoring me.

'It's got a hold. It's the cursed wind! Unless it drops, we'll all be burnt out of our houses!'

There came a banging at the door. A neighbour, Mr Harvey, rushed in.

'Fish Street Hill is all gone, John. St Magnus is burnt out, and the bridge is ablaze!'

The shoemaker banged his fist on the table.

'They should be pulling houses down in its path. What is the mayor doing?'

Mr Harvey shook his head.

'What do you think? He is taking his breakfast!'

Seething Lane
2nd September 1666
9 a.m.

I was the only servant that lived in at Mrs
Shaw's house. Her other servant, Mary,
walked there each day from Thames Street.
Nine o'clock came and there was no sign
of her, so I prepared Mrs Shaw's breakfast
myself. She was still worried.

'Go out in the street, Martha,' she said
to me when she had finished her breakfast.
'Seek out news of the fire.'

I put on my bonnet and shawl and went
out. The sun was already hot, though a
huge column of black smoke darkened the
sky to the west. Who could I ask? I was
timid by nature, and found it hard to speak

to strangers. I walked up Seething Lane towards the Navy Office. There I saw my friend Jane, Mr Pepys' servant. She was full of news about the fire, although she knew little more than I did.

'Mr Pepys went to the Tower this morning to see the fire from one of the high places there. He sent word he will not be home. He has gone to Whitehall, to speak with the King.'

'Are we in danger, Jane? Mrs Shaw is very frightened.'

'Mr Hewer says the fire is moving away from us, because of the wind. He thinks the soldiers will soon start blowing up houses in Eastcheap with gunpowder, and that will be an end to it. There is nothing for us to fear, Martha – it will never get this far, I am sure.'

The fire was moving west. I thought of

my brother, and the little shoemaker's shop
in Cannon Street. It was only a street away
from Eastcheap.

Cannon Street
2nd September 1666
11 a.m.

Usually all of my master's household would have been in church that morning, but that day the congregation at St Swithin's was small. All of the shopkeepers in Cannon Street were packing up their belongings. At about ten o'clock Mayor Bludworth passed by, on his way back from the fire. He was filthy, and wore an old handkerchief round his neck, not at all like the grand figure we sometimes saw riding past.

My master, Mr Harvey, and others begged him to order that more houses be pulled down, to make an empty space the fire could not cross, but he just looked helpless.

'What can I do? I am spent; people will not obey me. I have been pulling down houses, but the fire overtakes us faster than we can do it!'

So we started packing up everything of value in the shop. Mr Brown had a mind to move it all to his uncle's house, far out in the country at Stepney. But the fire was in the way, and the streets to the north were crowded with people fleeing the city. The only way was by boat.

Mr Brown had been down to the river, where he and Mr Harvey knew a boatman who kept a lighter at Dowgate Dock. When they returned they were in an angry mood. It seemed everyone in London was looking to hire boats and my master and Mr Harvey had to agree to pay twenty pounds then and there if they were to secure the lighter.

They had little choice. Already much of
Thames Street was ablaze. My master had
a small cart, and we all pitched in to load
it. Mr Harvey earned his living by copying
documents, and his stock in trade was
small. Even so, I knew that it would take at
least three journeys from Cannon Street to
Dowgate Dock before everything was
moved. And all this time it was more and
more difficult to move. The streets were
crowded with people, loading carts and the
backs of horses, piling belongings on their
own backs, shifting goods from one street to
another in a hopeless attempt to save them
from the fire. If we stood still for a second
we could hear the roaring of the flames,
and drops of fire were already beginning to
fall from the sky. The air was choking, and
pained our lungs. And all the time I
thought of nothing but my poor sister, away

in the east. How was she faring on this most terrible of days?

Seething Lane
2nd September 1666
4-8 p.m.

Mrs Shaw was much comforted by my report of the fire. She thought very highly of Mr Pepys.

'If Mr Pepys has been to the King, and told him of the fire, then action will be taken,' she said. 'Mr Pepys is a clever man. He will know what is best to do.'

I saw Jane again later, and she told me that Mr Pepys had returned home. The news from the City was bad, and London Bridge was well ablaze, but Mr Pepys had refused to cancel the dinner party he had arranged for that evening. I passed this on to Mrs Shaw, and she was well pleased.

If Mr. Pepys felt secure in his house, then so did she.

It was a worrying day for Mrs Shaw, and she took to her bed early. This was a long proceeding, for I had to bring water so that she could wash herself as she sat in her chair, then help her remove her day clothes and dress her in her nightgown and night cap. At last she was settled. I went downstairs and lit a candle, for I had a basket of mending to attend to.

As I sat next to the open window, I noticed, for the first time, the smell of smoke in the air.

Dowgate Dock
2nd September 1666
6 p.m.

'Take care lad! You'll have it over!'

The lighter was packed high with goods. Mrs Brown and her maid Elizabeth were already on board, squeezed between two sacks of new shoe leather. Mr Harvey was just clambering in. I was struggling with a bag of workshop tools, but it was difficult to find a place for them. A small space was left at the back, just enough for my master, the boatman and me.

The fire was hot on our faces. The steelyard, just two hundred yards downriver, was already burning. At this rate, the dockside where we were standing would be ablaze within the hour.

The river was crowded with boats, with people fleeing upstream, downstream, any direction just to get away from the fire. Barrels, boxes and all manner of other goods that had fallen from boats bobbed about on waves that flickered eerily in the reflection of the flames. We were all filthy from the smoke and ashes that drifted down on us. And still the wind taunted us, blowing steadily from the east; a 'Belgian wind' people called it.

There was a *whoomph!* And the roof on the building next to the dock caught fire, and blazing straw blew all around us like a million red stars.

'We must go now!' The old boatman shouted over the roar of the flames. 'The fire is upon us! Everything will be lost!' Just at that moment my master arrived.

On his shoulders was a huge sack of goods rescued from the shop.

'There's no room for it,' the old boatman shouted. 'Leave it behind, man! It'll capsize us!'

But my master wouldn't leave it. He climbed into the boat and dumped the huge sack into the only remaining space. My space.

I looked down and realised what this meant.

'Master! What about me?'

The shoemaker didn't even look at me.

'You can see there's no room. You must shift for yourself. Boatman, push off, before we are all burnt to cinders.'

And the boat disappeared into the smoke that floated down the river, leaving me on the dockside. For a moment I stood, unable to decide what to do; but I was brought to

my senses by a great, rending crash, as
burning beams from the building next to
the dock crashed down behind me. I turned
to run, but the narrow alleyway that led up
to the street was now a mass of flames.

Seething Lane
2nd September 1666
11 p.m.

I went up to bed at 10 o'clock, but I couldn't sleep. Usually, the street was quiet after dark, but I could still hear the sound of shouting and carts in the streets. The thought of the fire frightened me. What could I do? I was sure I could not get Mrs Shaw down the stairs on my own. Everyone else would be too busy to help. I could escape easily, but how could I leave Mrs Shaw to burn to death?

There was more noise from below, and I opened my window and looked out. My window overlooked the garden of our neighbours, Mr and Mrs Turner. Everything was dark this side of the house, but I could hear voices, and the sound of digging. Later I learned that they were burying their valuables, in case their house was lost, but at the time I did not know this. The sound brought back horrible memories of last year, the year of the plague. I couldn't hear digging now without thinking of graves.

I went to check that Mrs Shaw was comfortable. She was sleeping peacefully, even though there was noise in the street. Outside, the whole sky was glowing red, and I saw flames shooting up – much nearer than last night. If only Martin were here. But he was away in the City, on the other side of that terrible wall of flame.

Lombard Street
Monday 3rd September 1666
7 a.m.

I did not wake up until seven o'clock.
At first I did not know where I was, then
I remembered the struggle to take all my
master's goods to Dowgate Dock, and how
he had abandoned me there, too late even
to escape from the dockside. How I had
yelled and danced about! Then a kindly
family travelling upstream in a crowded boat
took me on board as far as Queenhythe, and
I was safe for the time being.

When I got there I had no idea what was
the best thing to do, so I decided to return
to Cannon Street. I had a few belongings
of my own, but I had left them behind, as

there was no room for them on the boat.

The streets were still packed with people moving down to the river, and moving out into the countryside to the west. I looked east as I crossed Thames Street, and saw a monstrous wall of flame. No one was trying to fight it. How could they? Already the roofs of nearby building were beginning to smoulder as falling sparks started small fires.

It was hard work moving against the flow of people. Some of the smaller lanes were blocked from wall to wall with carts; men were shouting, women screaming, children crying. The old and sick were carried along on stretchers; once I saw a father struggling to carry a heavy cradle with a sick child in it.

When I finally reached Cannon Street the fire was within a hundred yards of the shop, and I guessed that within an hour it would be gone. I rushed to the door, but, of course, my master had locked it. I thought about breaking open a shutter and climbing in, but I didn't want to be taken for a thief and thrown into prison for the sake of my few possessions.

I moved north then, away from the fire, towards the centre of the City. I was thinking about Martha, alone in that house with the old lady she looked after. My intention was to make my way to Seething Lane by way of Fenchurch Street. Then I realised how tired I was. My lungs were full of smoke, and every breath was painful. I had to fight to take each step forward.

As I passed the churchyard of St Mary's I began to feel faint. There was a roaring in my head like that of the fire itself. The churchyard was cool, and dark, and I decided to rest myself there for just a moment, and fell into a sleep.

And that was where I found myself when I awoke the next morning, stretched out on some poor fellow's grave. I thought that my head was still roaring, but as I woke properly I realised that the sound was really the fire, burning just a few streets away. Had I slept for another hour, I would have been burnt to death.

Seething Lane
3rd September 1666
11 a.m.

Mary did not come again that morning.
Outside, the sky was dark, and the street
filthy with fallen ashes. I knew the fire
was coming closer, but I couldn't tell
Mrs Shaw this.

I slipped out and saw Jane. She told
me that Mr Pepys had taken his gold to
Bethnal Green early in the morning, but
that he did not think the fire would reach
Seething Lane. That comforted me a little.
As we spoke, a number of loud explosions
went off, and Jane told me that soldiers had
finally got round to blowing up houses away
in the City to stop the fire spreading.

Cornhill, London
3rd September 1666
Noon

When I left the churchyard that morning
I turned east. But when I reached the
crossroads at Gracechurch Street I saw the
road ahead was completely blocked with
the carts of rich merchants, frantically
loading their belongings, or trying to shift
their carts away. Some carts had
overturned, while others had become
wedged together so no movement was
possible. At one point the road had been
dug up to reach the water pipes, and the
wheels of the carts were stuck in the hole.
I looked down Gracechurch Street towards
Fish Street Hill, and saw the fire advancing

apace. I could not imagine that the crush of carts and people and goods could be cleared before the flames reached it.

I resolved to go further north, and work my way round to Seething Lane by way of Aldgate. But when I reached Cornhill I found a great company of the King's Guards setting charges to blow up houses there, and a grand figure on a horse urging them on. I had seen him before, in a royal procession in Cheapside; it was the King's own son, the Duke of Monmouth. Although he was proudly dressed, and in charge of many men, in truth he was very little older than I was.

He called to me.

'You, fellow. Take this message at once to the fire post in Coleman Street. If any stop you, show them the letter and say you are on the King's business!'

He passed me down a piece of paper, with a gold coin inside; I thought myself well paid for the short journey, even though it took me out of my way.

Short journey it is, but with the crush in the streets, it took me over an hour to reach the fire post; there I saw a weary-looking parish constable sitting on a bench outside, and I gave him my message, telling him it came from the Duke. It turned out that the constable couldn't read, and so a harassed-looking magistrate was sent for.

'He asks when the militia are to be expected. But how am I to know?'

He took the paper into the fire post, found a pen, and scribbled a reply.

'Here. Take this reply to the Duke.'

I waited hopefully for another coin, but none was forthcoming this time, so unwillingly, I set off to return to Cornhill.

But the fire had already reached there, and although many houses had been blown up, or pulled down, that achieved nothing, for the fire simply spread along the timbers left lying in the road.

I saw no sign of the Duke, and the soldiers did not know where he was. I decided to resume my journey east.

Newgate Prison
3rd September 1666
8 p.m.

My downfall came as I tried to work my way along Threadneedle Street. I met many soldiers on my way, pulling back from the fire, weary and dispirited. And then a man came rushing out of an alley pushing a cart, loaded with goods, with a baby asleep on it. He stopped when he saw me.

'Stand by the cart for me, lad. I have left something behind. I'll reward you!'

If I had used my wits, I would have realised something was wrong when he ran off in a completely different direction; but I stood there holding the handles of the cart. Then out of the alleyway came a screaming

woman and a man with a face of thunder.
The man grabbed me and started to beat
me, accusing me of stealing all he had, and
the woman took up the baby and pinched
it to make it cry to make sure I had not
murdered it. And a sergeant in uniform
came along and asked what was to do.

'This young thief has tried to steal all
we had.'

'He took my child!'

Despite all I could do or say no one
would believe my story of the runaway
thief. The soldier said the magistrates
had told them to deal harshly with thieves,
and my hands were tied up and I was
marched away.

I tried to tell them that I was innocent,
and that I was a messenger on the King's
business, but the soldiers just laughed. It
had to be said that I didn't look like a royal

messenger. And all the time I had the note signed by the Duke in my pocket, but, as my hands were tied, I could not show it to them. They would probably have thought that I had stolen that as well.

The soldiers were marching to the west to take up positions there, so they took me to the prison at Newgate, and handed me over to the turnkey. He looked at me in disgust. He was only interested in prisoners with money, and I certainly didn't look like a rich man, but when he searched my pockets and found my gold coin, he looked on me with greater favour.

'So, master thief, where did you come by this?'

'The Duke of Monmouth gave it to me. See. I have a letter from him.'

But the turnkey didn't believe my unlikely story, and couldn't read in any case; so I was thrown into a stinking dungeon crowded with men, many drunk and all violent, to spend the night as best I could, with the cheerful prospect of harsh justice and a hanging to come.

Seething Lane
Tuesday 4th September 1666
4 p.m.

All day I heard news from neighbours of the
fire creeping closer and closer. Jane told me
that most of the City had been destroyed,
and that St Paul's itself was threatened.
Somehow, I had to get Mrs Shaw out of the
house. But she refused to even try. It seemed
that now even the thought of the flames
could not drive her from her room.

'It is God's will, Martha,' she said. 'The
city is a place of sin. We are all sinners. I
will wait here, Martha, for God's judgement.
But you are a good, innocent girl. Leave me!
Save yourself. Go now, quickly!'

But I refused. Although I feared the fire,

I could not bear to leave the old lady alone to die. So all that long day I prepared her meals, and sat with her sewing or reading aloud; while outside the smoke grew darker and the flames brighter.

Ludgate Hill
4th September 1666
8 p.m.

I escaped!

It happened this way. By late afternoon it was decided that the prison itself was lost. All prisoners were mustered outside to be moved to Lambeth, across the river. For some of the prisoners, it was the first daylight they had seen for many days.

A guard of soldiers formed around us, and the order to march was given. But the guard was few in number and the prisoners desperate; some men in front of me rushed at the soldiers, and tried to grab their weapons, and a great to-do started. I found myself opposite a small alleyway halfway down Old Bailey, and while the guards were distracted I slipped into it. Within seconds I was slipping through a maze of passageways.

But where was I to go from here? The fire raged to the east. I could not safely go west, back into Old Bailey, in case I was recognised. So I worked my way south, and reached Ludgate Hill at about seven o'clock.

And there I saw the most horrible, hellish sight of all. St Paul's itself was blazing, and the very lead from its roof was melting and pouring down Ludgate Hill towards me like a mighty waterfall of fire. Even the great stones of the cathedral themselves were exploding in the heat, like cannon in battle. To the south, the fire was still spreading along the riverside. The wall of fire was only minutes away from where I stood. Turning north again, I ran for my life.

Seething Lane
Wednesday 5th September 1666
8 a.m.

It was an anxious night. I was awoken at
2 a.m. by a knocking on the door. It was
Jane. She told me that the fire was burning
down all of Tower Street and that Mrs Pepys
and the servants were leaving that instant
for Woolwich.

'You must leave with your mistress as
soon as you can, Martha,' she told me. 'Mr
Pepys fears the whole street will be lost!'

So saying, she left me.

I sat up for the rest of the night. It would
be difficult enough to move Mrs Shaw
during daylight, when she was fully awake;
at night it would be impossible. I was

determined to make Mrs Shaw see reason. Somehow, I needed to force her to make the dangerous journey down the stairs and out into the street before the flames reached the house. But how?

I took up her breakfast as usual. She was already awake, and I saw that she had been writing. She ate her food, slowly, slowly; and all the time I imagined the fire was licking at the very front door.

Then I opened her window. Immediately, the smell of smoke came into the room.

'Madam, we must go. The fire is nearly upon us. If we leave it any longer, we shall both perish.'

Mrs Shaw looked at me. For the first time, I saw a look of kindness in her face.

'Martha, I am resigned to it. I am an old woman, and my time has come. Take this paper and leave me.'

But I wouldn't leave the mistress I had served for over three years. I sat down in her chair.

'I will not leave the house without you, Ma'am.'

She knew that I meant what I said.

'Very well,' she said. 'For your sake I will try. But I must be dressed properly if I am to appear in the street.'

So, with the fire raging closer and closer, I helped her out of her bedclothes, and washed her, and put on her layers of day clothes. With each layer, my heart sank. How could I get her down the narrow stairs?

At last she was ready. I helped her from her chair and opened the bedroom door. More smoke came up from an open window below. With her hand on the wall, she lowered her foot onto the first stair. Then, with a little moan, she clutched her head, slipped, and collapsed.

She did not fall or slide down the stairs because of the bend in them, but lay there on the steps in a great heap. At first I thought her dead, but her hand and face were twitching. At that moment there came a thunderous knocking at the door.

Mrs Shaw blocked the stairs completely. I called out, but I did not think whoever was at the door could hear me. I did not have time to wonder why someone was knocking. I tried all I could to revive the old lady, even returning to her room to throw water in her face.

At last the moaning stopped, and I knew that she was dead.

And then came another wild knocking at the door, and I called out again that I was there. Then there was a great battering of someone smashing it down. The door fell

open, and smoke poured in, and I thought
my last hour had come.

Seething Lane
5th September 1666
8 a.m.

I walked all night, and I was exhausted.
I had managed to reach Holborn, beyond
the fire. At first I could think of nothing
but escape, but at last I was able to think
more clearly. I decided to walk in a great
loop around London. I trudged along
outside the wall, and finally reached
Moorfields at dawn. Here it seemed the
whole of London was camped out under the
stars. There I entered the City again, and
found everything was a smoking ruin. Some
fires still burned, for many people kept oil
and such things in their cellars.

The ground was scorching hot, and my

poor shoes did little to protect my feet.
I soon lost my way, for everything was
changed. I headed towards the dawn glow,
knowing that way I was moving east, and at
last came to where the fire had burnt itself
out, and I knew where I was. It was the
church of St Martin Outwich! I had reached
the parish that had taken my sister and I in
when we were abandoned as babies. By a
miracle, the church had survived the fire.
Of all the sights I saw at that time, the sight
of my old church still standing was the one
that made me weep the most.

Aldgate was just a short way off, but the
smoke and ashes had overcome me again.
Finding an abandoned cart in the street, I
lay on it and slept awhile.

When I woke the sun was up, glowing
redly in the east through the smoky air. I
set off once more. At last, with my feet

scorched and bleeding from the hot ashes,
I turned past St Olave's and into Seething
Lane. At the far end nearest the river I
could see flames, just two doors away from
Mrs Shaw's house. And outside a group of
men were placing a barrel against the wall.
I knew at once that it was gunpowder.

Despite my poor burnt feet, I rushed
down the lane to the house, begging them
not to fire the charges.

Two important-looking men were in
charge. One was Mrs Shaw's neighbour, Mr
Pepys. The other, I found out later, was Sir
William Penn.

'What is it?' said Mr Pepys. 'We have
urgent business here if the rest of the street
is to be saved.'

'My sister and her employer! They may
still be inside! Old Mrs Shaw was unable to
leave her room, and I am sure my sister

would not leave her.'

Sir William looked impatient.

'We have knocked, and there was no sound from within. There is no one in the house.'

I needed to be certain. I hammered again on the door and listened; and heard a faint voice calling. This time, the other men heard it too. Between us, we had the door down, and rushed in. At first, all we could see was a large pair of feet on the stairs; then, above them, the anxious, weeping face of my sister Martha.

Seething Lane
5th September 1666
10 a.m.

And so Martin came just in time to stop
the house being blown up around my ears;
and Mr Pepys himself came into the house
and helped me down over the body of my
poor employer. And then came the greatest
miracle of all. Mr Pepys was all for blowing
up the house then and there, with the poor
body of Mrs Shaw still inside it; but one of
the men called to him.

'Sir! Look around you! The wind has
changed! It is blowing south, towards the
river! The fire is dying down! It's over, sir!'
And so it was. The Great Fire (for that was
what we called it in the years that

followed) stopped, on that Wednesday morning, just two doors away from that house in Seething Lane.

And so Martin and I stood in the road, he with his poor scorched clothes and burnt feet, both wondering what would become of us; but by then the men had managed to ease Mrs Shaw's poor corpse down the stairs, and Mr Pepys noticed the paper she had been writing clutched in her hands.

He took it and read it, then turned to me.

'Your name is Martha Outwich? Mrs Shaw speaks here of your great loyalty to her. This paper is her will, my dear. Be thankful that the house was not destroyed, for it, and all her possessions, are now yours.'

I could not take it all in at first, so he showed the document to me

'But sir,' I said. 'If this is a true will, should it not be witnessed? There is no signature on it but hers.'

Mr Pepys called for a pen to be brought to him, and signed the will himself.

'And should anyone say it is not a true will, they will have me to answer to!'

Epilogue

It turned out that Mrs Shaw was richer than anyone had thought, and we were well set for the rest of our lives. We lived together in Mrs Shaw's house, and Mr. Pepys helped us manage our affairs at first.

We were determined not to spend our time in idleness. The city was in ruins, and it was our duty to help; especially the poor of our own parish of St Martin Outwich, that had fed us and clothed us, and given us our names.

What next?

Visit *Fire's* own interactive website

www.fireinteractive.co.uk

And explore

• The historical background to the story

• Information on the characters and places

• Diaries by Samuel Pepys and others
writing at the time of the fire

And much more!

Blitz - David Orme

It's World War II and Martin has been
evacuated to the country. He hates it so much,
he runs back home to London. But home isn't
where it used to be…

Gateway from Hell - John Banks

Lisa and her friends are determined to stop the
new road being built. Especially as it means
digging up Mott Hill. Because something
ancient lies beneath the hill. Something
dangerous - something *deadly*…

Cry Baby - Jill Atkins

Charlie is fifteen and in her last year at school.
Her dad makes too much fuss about the clothes
she wears, but Charlie knows how to handle
herself. Or so she thinks…

Doing the Double - Alan Durant

Dale and Joe are twins. They've always laughed
about doing the double – swapping identities for
the day. It's always been a joke - until now…

Fighting Back - Helen Bird

After her father's business is destroyed in a fire, Amita and her family move to Southampton to start a new life. Everything will be better there…

Hunter's Moon - John Townsend

Neil loves working as a gamekeeper. But something very strange is going on in the woods… What is the meaning of the message Neil receives? And why should he beware the Hunter's Moon?

A Murder of Crows - Penny Bates

Ben is new to the country, and when he makes friends with a lonely crow, finds himself being bullied. Now the bullies want him to hurt his only friend. But they have reckoned without the power of crow law…

Nightmare Park - Philip Preece

Dreamland… a place where your dreams come true. Or do they?

Plague - David Orme

Plague has come to the city of London. For Henry Harper, life will never be the same. His father is dead, and his family have fled. Henry must find a way to escape from the city he loves, before he, too, is struck down…

Space Explorers - David Johnson

Sammi and Zak have been stranded on a strange planet, surrounded by deadly spear plants. Luckily mysterious horned-creatures rescue them. Now all they need to do is get back to their ship…

Tears of a Friend - Joanna Kenrick

Cassie and Claire have been friends for ever. Cassie thinks nothing will ever split them apart. But then, the unthinkable happens. They have a row, and now Cassie feels so alone. What can she do to mend a friendship? Or has she lost Claire … for good?

The Messenger - John Townsend

Chris doesn't take any notice when a piece of glass angel smashes in front of him. Particularly when a stranger tells him it's a warning...

Treachery by Night - Ann Ruffell

Glencoe, 1692

Conn longs to be a brave warrior, just like his cousin Jamie. But what kind of warrior has a withered arm?

Who Cares? - Helen Bird

Tara hates her life – till she meets Liam, and things start looking up. Only, Liam doesn't approve of Tara taking drugs. But Tara won't listen. She can handle it. Or can she?